™

www.mascotbooks.com

For more information, please contact:
Mascot Books
560 Herndon Parkway #120
Herndon, VA 20170
info@mascotbooks.com

CPSIA Code: PRT1015A
ISBN-13: 9781620869666

Printed in the United States

LET'S GO, NORTH DAKOTA!

Gordon P. Kushner

Illustrated by **Danny Moore**

It was a beautiful fall day at the University of North Dakota. Two University of North Dakota alumni were showing their children around campus.

The whole family was excited for the evening's
hockey game.

The first thing the family did was visit Clifford Hall. Dad said,
"This is where I took my Aerospace Science classes."

Some students passed by and called, "Let's go, North Dakota!"

Mom suggested, "Let's show the kids the library where we used to study."

They headed to Chester Fritz Library, the largest library in North Dakota. UND students were studying at tables. "Let's go, North Dakota," whispered the students.

Next the family stopped at the Soaring Eagle Statue to enjoy the scenery. There were several students reading on the grass.

As they passed, the family said, "Let's go, North Dakota!"

"My belly is rumbling. Let's get something to eat at
the Memorial Union!" Dad exclaimed.

The family ate a delicious and nutritious meal. Some students
sat down with them and said, "Let's go, North Dakota!"

From the Union, the family strolled down University Avenue where fraternity and sorority students were doing volunteer work.

The students waved to them and called, "Let's go, North Dakota! See you at the game!"

Finally, the family arrived at Ralph Englestad Arena – home of the University of North Dakota Ice Hockey Team.

UND fans were excited for the game. The family was happy to join in the excitement. Fans wearing green, white, and black cheered, "Let's go, North Dakota!"

It was time for the University of North Dakota
hockey team to take the ice.

As the team skated out the players cheered, "Let's go, North Dakota!"

The family watched the game from the stands and cheered
for the home team. North Dakota scored!

"Goal!" called the team's captain as he skated to the bench.

The game was tied with less than five minutes to play. The family knew
supporting the team would help, so they decided to get the crowd going.
They got everyone singing the University of North Dakota fight song
"Stand Up and Cheer".

The center scored with one minute left!

North Dakota won!

The hockey team played hard and beat their rivals!
The players and coaches celebrated the victory!

The family gave the players high-fives as they
left the rink. Everyone cheered.

The family was thrilled with the big win. As they left the arena, fans cheered, "Let's go, North Dakota!"

After the game, the children were tired. It had been a long day at the University of North Dakota. As soon as they got home, the kids crawled into bed. They asked their parents, "Can we go to the University of North Dakota when we grow up?"

Their parents smiled and said, "Of course you can. Goodnight."

The End.

Have a book idea?

Contact us at:

Mascot Books
560 Herndon Parkway #120
Herndon, VA 20170

info@mascotbooks.com | www.mascotbooks.com

UND®